This book belongs to:

_____

The Challah Girl

Written by **Bracha K. Sharp**

Illustrated by **Anita Tung**

For my parents
and to my maternal and paternal grandparents,
of blessed memory, with love—this one's for you!

B.K.S.

My deepest gratitude to those who have helped bring my picture book into creation:

Valerie Stark, for calling me "a challah girl" when we sold challahs together.

Professor Michael Popkin, for always encouraging me, and whose course on fairy tales and the psychology behind them inspired me to set the scene in those lands.

My family, friends, and fellow-writers, who reviewed the manuscript.

My illustrator, Anita Tung, whose beautiful work shines through.

And, last but certainly not least, the wonderful staff at Mosaica Press for their kindness, creativity, and patience.

Above all, my thanks goes to Hashem, the Creator of the Universe, from Whose kindness and love all inspiration and abilities flow.

BRACHA K. SHARP is an author, writer, and poet. She draws particular inspiration from her background in English literature and psychology, poetry, nature, folklore and myth, and her favorite childhood books. When not writing, she loves to spend time with her family, friends, and literary character-named guinea pigs; attend book conventions; and occasionally bake challahs, which she hopes turn out as good as Zlatah Leah's!

ANITA TUNG is an illustrator living and working in the California Bay Area. Her work is heavily influenced by the natural world and often conveys a sense of exploration and wonder. She blends digital and traditional processes and enjoys experimentation with physical media, particularly painting and printmaking. The primary goal of her work is to present viewers with strange and unknown things in a way that prompts curiosity.

© 2019 by Mosaica Press. All rights reserved

ISBN-10: 1-946351-62-8   ISBN-13: 978-1-946351-62-3

No part of this publication may be translated, reproduced, stored in a retrieval system or transmitted in any form or by any means, electronic, mechanical, photocopying, recording, or otherwise, without prior permission in writing from both the copyright holder and the publisher.

Published and distributed by: Mosaica Press, Inc.
www.mosaicapress.com   info@mosaicapress.com

nce, a very, very long time ago, before you or I were just a twinkle in our parents' eyes, there was a small Jewish town right in the middle of two mountains. At the top of one of the mountains was the royal palace, and in the center of the valley was where the people lived, worked, and prayed.

In one of the thatched cottages, a young girl named Zlatah Leah lived with her brothers, sisters, parents, and grandparents.

Zlatah Leah was good at sewing and churning milk into butter. She could play ball as well as any of her brothers, and—to the delight of her siblings—she could pick the apples off the highest branches of the tree growing in their front yard.

But most of all, Zlatah Leah was known for the challahs that she made.

"They are the best challahs in the land," declared her mother.

"Our Sabbath would feel incomplete without them," said her father.

From one end of the little village and back, the neighbors came to ask Zlatah Leah for her recipe. However, when they tried to copy it, their own challahs never turned out as fine or as tasty as Zlatah Leah's.

One day, after the villagers had successfully harvested their grain, they brought their bounty to the mill to grind it into flour.

Suddenly, a scarlet-robed messenger from the palace clattered into town, passing right by the mill. He was headed to the rabbi's house, located in the center of the village.

person from the palace in royal livery! What on earth could be wrong? The stunned villagers ran after him.

Zlatah Leah and her family ran after the crowd. They joined the other villagers who were standing by the rabbi's open windows, listening in rapt silence.

Honored Rabbi," said the messenger, bowing low. "I have come because of Prince Isaac. The king and queen are beside themselves with worry," and he dropped his voice to a whisper, "because the prince no longer laughs or smiles! The royal couple has tried everything—but to no avail."

"Hmm," said the rabbi. "Are you saying that he does not laugh or smile although his very name, Isaac, means laughter?"

"That is indeed the problem, Rabbi!" said the messenger. "Why, up until the harvest, he was constantly smiling. The wise men have tried all sorts of things—but nothing has worked. And so the king and queen have sent me to you."

"Ahh…but what happened after the harvest?" questioned the rabbi, going over to his shelves and consulting some holy books. "And what did the wise men suggest?"

The messenger answered, "Nobody knows what happened. The first wise man said that our prince should stand on his head in order to move his thoughts about. But that only caused him a headache. The second wise man said that he should drink an infusion of saltwater in order to prompt him to cry and thereby release his sadness. He did not cry, but he did feel ill. And the third wise man suggested that everyone including the palace jester should tell him jokes. But after he laughed, he went right back to sighing."

"Tell me," said the Rabbi, "does his sadness exist every day? On holidays? On the Sabbath?"

"Honored Rabbi," the messenger responded, "I will investigate and return to you with more information." He bowed once more and took his leave.

wo days later, the rabbi and his students went to knock on all of the cottage doors. They had important news from the palace.

"The prince does not laugh like he used to—not even on the Sabbath! In fact, on the Sabbath, he eats less and sighs more. Nobody, not even the prince, knows why.

"So, with my blessing, the king and queen have requested that any villager who feels he can help should go to the royal palace and present the prince with something that will make him smile again."

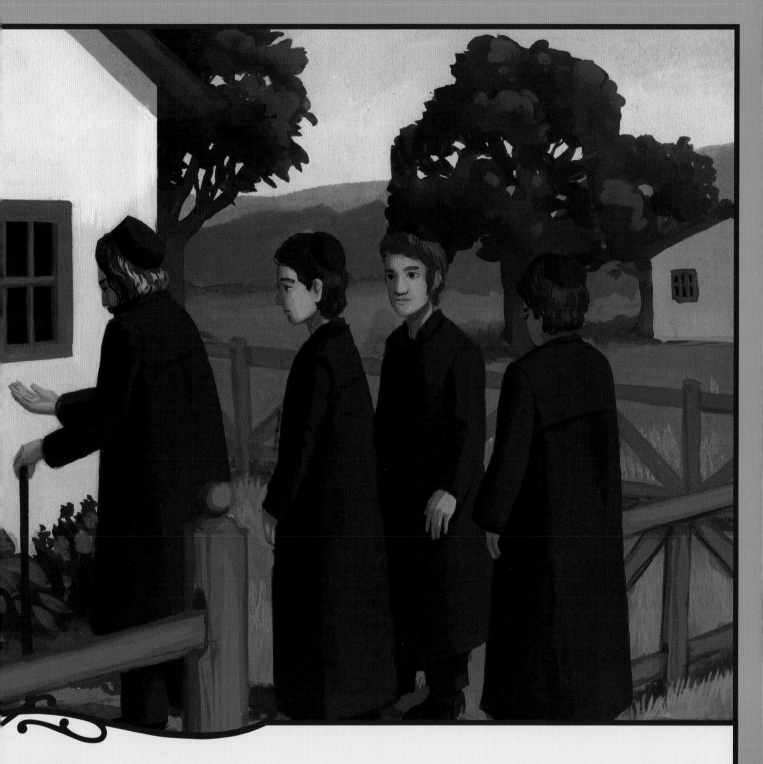

Zlatah Leah thought long and hard about what to do. Finally, at nightfall, she told her parents that she would go to the palace tomorrow to try to make the prince smile again.

"You have many fine talents, Zlatah Leah," her father said, "but what can you do that will make him smile?"

"Well," said Zlatah Leah, "I can make my challah for him!"

"What use has he for your challah, Zlatah Leah," said her mother, "when he already has many bakers to make challah for him whenever he wants?"

"But he hasn't tried *my* challahs yet," Zlatah Leah said. "And you've always said that they are the best in the land!"

And so, early the next morning, her family bid her goodbye—and good luck. Zlatah Leah rode off on her donkey, with an apple in one apron pocket and a sack of ingredients in the other.

The path up the hill to the royal palace was bumpy and steep, and Zlatah Leah held onto the donkey's mane. Suddenly, the donkey stumbled over a rock...and out fell the sack of ingredients from her apron pocket!

 alf of the flour spilled out onto the path. Zlatah Leah gasped. She bent down to retrieve the sack and saw that there was only enough flour to make a very small loaf of challah.

Zlatah Leah could not help but cry. But she soon wiped her tears, put the sack back into her apron pocket, and rode on.

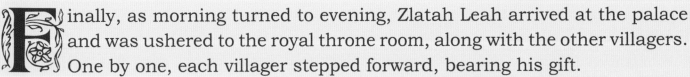

Finally, as morning turned to evening, Zlatah Leah arrived at the palace and was ushered to the royal throne room, along with the other villagers. One by one, each villager stepped forward, bearing his gift.

One villager told the prince that he would make him a fine sword, and another villager said that she would make him a wonderful purple and crimson vest with two pockets.

A third said that he would make his special rhubarb pie. And one by one, they were thanked and then dismissed, until only Zlatah Leah and eleven other villagers were told to stay.

The king and queen asked Zlatah Leah what she could do for the prince. She held up her half-filled flour sack and proudly told them that she was known for making the best challahs in the land.

"Is this so?" said the king.

"Are you, indeed?" questioned the queen.

Suddenly, the prince spoke up.

"A claim like that," he said thoughtfully, "must have some basis to it. Please stay and make me a challah for my dinner tonight."

nd so, in the royal kitchen, Zlatah Leah mixed her ingredients together to make a fine dough. She hoped the prince would like her challah. But when the loaf came out of the oven, it was no bigger than her two hands held together.

When Zlatah Leah was called forward to present her gift, a messenger brought the challah to the prince on a silver platter. The prince washed his hands, made the blessing, broke off a piece of challah, and popped it into his mouth. The rest of the royal family did the same.

"Delightful!" said the king.

"Mmm!" said the queen.

"Delicious!" cried the royal siblings.

But the prince only said, "Hmm…," and took another piece.

"Hmm," he said again.

"I can see why you claim to be the best challah-maker in the land. But this challah is much too small. Come back tomorrow, and make me another larger challah, please!"

o back down the mountain Zlatah Leah went, and finally, at night, she arrived home and told her parents what the prince had requested.

The next morning, Zlatah Leah once again packed a sack of ingredients and made sure to close it securely. She began her journey to the palace. But the mountain was rocky, and as her donkey clambered up, the sack fell to the ground. This time, the honey jar rolled onto the path and half of it oozed out.

latah Leah felt tears welling up in her eyes. She bent down, picked up the jar, and replaced the cover. Now the challah would not be as sweet as she wanted it to be. But she took a deep breath, sat up straight, and rode on toward the palace.

Once in the royal kitchen, Zlatah Leah kneaded her dough, poured in all the remaining honey, and added in some cinnamon. Then, she braided it into a beautiful large loaf. This time, she prayed that her challah would impress the royal family and make the prince smile again. She knew, after all, that her challah was the best in the land!

"Even better!" cried the king.

"A masterpiece!" said the queen.

"And so sweet and tasty!" exclaimed the prince's siblings.

"Well," said the prince, "it's certainly bigger than last time, and the taste is just right. It *does* taste just like a perfect challah should. But I think that there's one more thing missing. Please come back again tomorrow, and I'm sure you'll figure it out!"

And with that, Zlatah Leah had no choice but to go back down the mountain.

At home, she told her family that most of the villagers' gifts had not helped the prince, and that she was one of the few people left still trying to make the prince smile. Zlatah Leah's family wanted to help her, and they gave her advice.

"Another pinch of salt would not be amiss!" claimed her mother.

"More honey, Zlatah Leah!" said her father.

"Do not knead it too much!" suggested her grandparents.

And so, early the next morning, for the third and possibly last time, Zlatah Leah packed up her ingredients in a small pouch. This time, she placed it across her chest, so that nothing could be lost. Once more, she set off for the royal palace atop her trusted donkey.

When she arrived at the palace, only two other villagers were there with their gifts. This time, when she followed the messenger down to the royal kitchen, she was so worried that she wouldn't be able to figure out what was missing from the prince's challah that she began to cry.

But as Zlatah Leah cracked the eggs and mixed in the honey, she began to pray. She remembered how nice the prince had always been to the villagers, and she prayed for his wellbeing. As she stirred in the salt and spices, she began to feel more confident and prayed that he would be healed. And as she kneaded and rolled and shaped the dough and formed it into beautifully braided loaves, she whispered many prayers, and her tears fell into the dough.

However, when Zlatah Leah was called forward to present her gift once more, the prince shook his head and sighed. "Perhaps I will save these loaves for tonight, since it is Friday and the Sabbath will be this evening. Please enjoy the Sabbath with your own family. Thank you for trying to make me smile."

Zlatah Leah's throat felt like it was covered in sawdust. She swallowed hard, nodded her head, and left to go home.

That evening, Zlatah Leah and her family welcomed the Sabbath as they did each and every week. Her mother lit the candles and her father made the blessings on the wine and challah. The Sabbath was peaceful and calming—but Zlatah Leah could not help worrying about everything that she had put into the challah and if it had been enough to help the prince.

And so, that evening, when everybody was asleep, she prayed hard that she had done all she could do.

She knew that it was all in G-d's hands and part of His master plan.

arly on the day following the Sabbath, one of the king's messengers knocked on the cottage door. In a serious voice, he said that the prince had requested an audience with her.

Off they went, the messenger riding ahead on his horse and Zlatah Leah riding after him on her donkey—with nothing to hold except the hope that she carried in her heart.

When the queen saw her enter the throne room, she smiled, and the king began to clap. "Very good, Zlatah Leah!" he said.

"You have made our dear son laugh once more!" cried the queen.

And it was true. For there stood the prince—and he was smiling widely.

"It's a miracle!" said one of the king's wise men. "It's the bread!" said a second.

"Hush!" said the prince. Then, to Zlatah Leah he said, "Please—tell us your secret. On the first bite, I was pleased, on the second, I began to smile, and on the third, I began to laugh! I have not felt this happy for a long time."

Zlatah Leah smiled and curtsied, and then she shrugged. "Well, I just added water and flour, yeast and oil, eggs and some honey and spices—the usual!"

"But there must be a secret ingredient!" said the prince, looking confused. "Those are the ingredients, but what is the *secret* that you put into the dough?"

Zlatah Leah took a deep breath and thought hard for a moment.

"Well," she began, "the first time, I hoped you would like the taste of my challah. The next time, I wanted you to like how it looked. *This* time, as I kneaded the challah, I thought about how I wished you would be healed, and I began to pray for you. That's what I do whenever I make challah: I pray for my family—and for other things, too.

"So I guess I don't have any special ingredient. I just have my prayers and my tears, Your Majesties."

For a moment, everyone was silent.

And then the king began to laugh. "But of course, that's a special ingredient! Why, in fact it's *the* special ingredient that Prince Isaac was looking for! You see, you took the time to think of my son until you understood what he needed."

"Yes," said the queen. "It took great courage to keep trying until you succeeded!"

"I have an important announcement to make!" said the king. "We employ many fine chefs in the royal palace, but we have no one who can make challahs as fine as Zlatah Leah's. I would like you to be our Challah Girl."

The queen clapped her hands together. "And so would I!" she exclaimed.

Zlatah Leah curtsied, and the prince smiled.

From that day on, every single week, Zlatah Leah the Challah Girl baked her special challahs for the royal family. Time passed, and one day, the prince called her to the palace.

"Zlatah Leah," he said. "I have been thinking…someone whose prayers can make me smile is indeed…worthy of becoming my wife."

Zlatah Leah caught her breath and smiled. "Thank you, Your Highness," she said, "I am truly honored. However, I—"

"Yes?" said the prince.

"I—I would like some time to get to know the prince a bit better," Zlatah Leah blurted out. "Ah, yes," said Prince Isaac, "of course!"

And so it was.

A month's time passed, and a royal messenger was sent to tell the villagers that a royal wedding would be taking place—that of Prince Isaac and Zlatah Leah.

The prince knew that *now* he would always have reason to smile.

And that Zlatah Leah's challahs would bring G-d's blessings, far and wide, to all the land.